94
94

SAIL AWAY

Donald Crews

Greenwillow Books / New York

To the Seabiscuit,
captain and crew,
and to being here
to tell this tale

The full-color illustrations were created with Dr. Martin's Concentrated Water Colors applied with brush and airbrush. The text type is Akzidenz Grotesk Bold Italic.

Greenwillow Books, a division of William Morrow & Company, Inc., 1350 Avenue of the Americas, New York, NY 10019.
Printed in Singapore by Tien Wah Press
First Edition
10 9 8 7 6 5 4 3 2 1

Library of Congress Cataloging-in-Publication Data
Crews, Donald.
Sail away / by Donald Crews.
p. cm.
Summary: A family takes an enjoyable trip in their sailboat and watches the weather change throughout the day.
ISBN 0-688-11053-3 (trade).
ISBN 0-688-11054-1 (lib. bdg.)
[1. Sailing–Fiction.]
I. Title. PZ7.C8682Sai 1995 [E]–dc20 94-6004
CIP AC

A perfect day for sailing.

***We row the dinghy
out to our sailboat.***

Everything ready,
we motor from our mooring.
p u t t . . . p u t t . . . p u t t . . .

putt...putt...putt...

Under the bridge.

putt...putt...putt...

p u t t . . . p u t t . . . p u t t . . .
Past the lighthouse.
Motor off. p u t t . . . Sails up …

94
94

WHOO

Wind's up...

SAIL A

***Sail away
through the day.***

Sailing, sailing.
Clear skies turn
cloudy and gray.

Gray skies darken.
Seas swell.

Darker skies,
higher seas. . .
Angry
seas.
"Shorten sails!"

Sails down, we turn for home.

Calm again at last.
The sun is setting
as we motor toward port.

putt...putt...putt...

p u t t . . . p u t t . . . p u t t . . .

Past the lighthouse.

p u t t . . . p u t t . . . p u t t . . .

putt...putt...putt...

Under the bridge.

putt...putt...putt...

Moored!